A Bucket of Blessings

Kabir Sehgal & Surishtha Sehgal

Illustrated by
Jing Jing Tsong

Beach Lane Books • New York London Toronto Sydney New Delhi

Near a majestic mountain, in a vast jungle
with many mango trees, lives Monkey.
It has not rained for weeks.
The village well and the pond are dry.

Monkey and his neighbors look everywhere for water.

But no luck.

Then Monkey remembers a story his mama used to tell him—a story about how peacocks can make it rain by dancing.

So he decides to climb the nearby
mountain to visit Peacock.

But Peacock does not have good news.
"Oh, Monkey, I need water to make it rain," he says.
"Can you find me some?"
Monkey isn't sure. But he says he'll try.

On his way back down the mountain,
Monkey stops to cool off in a cave.

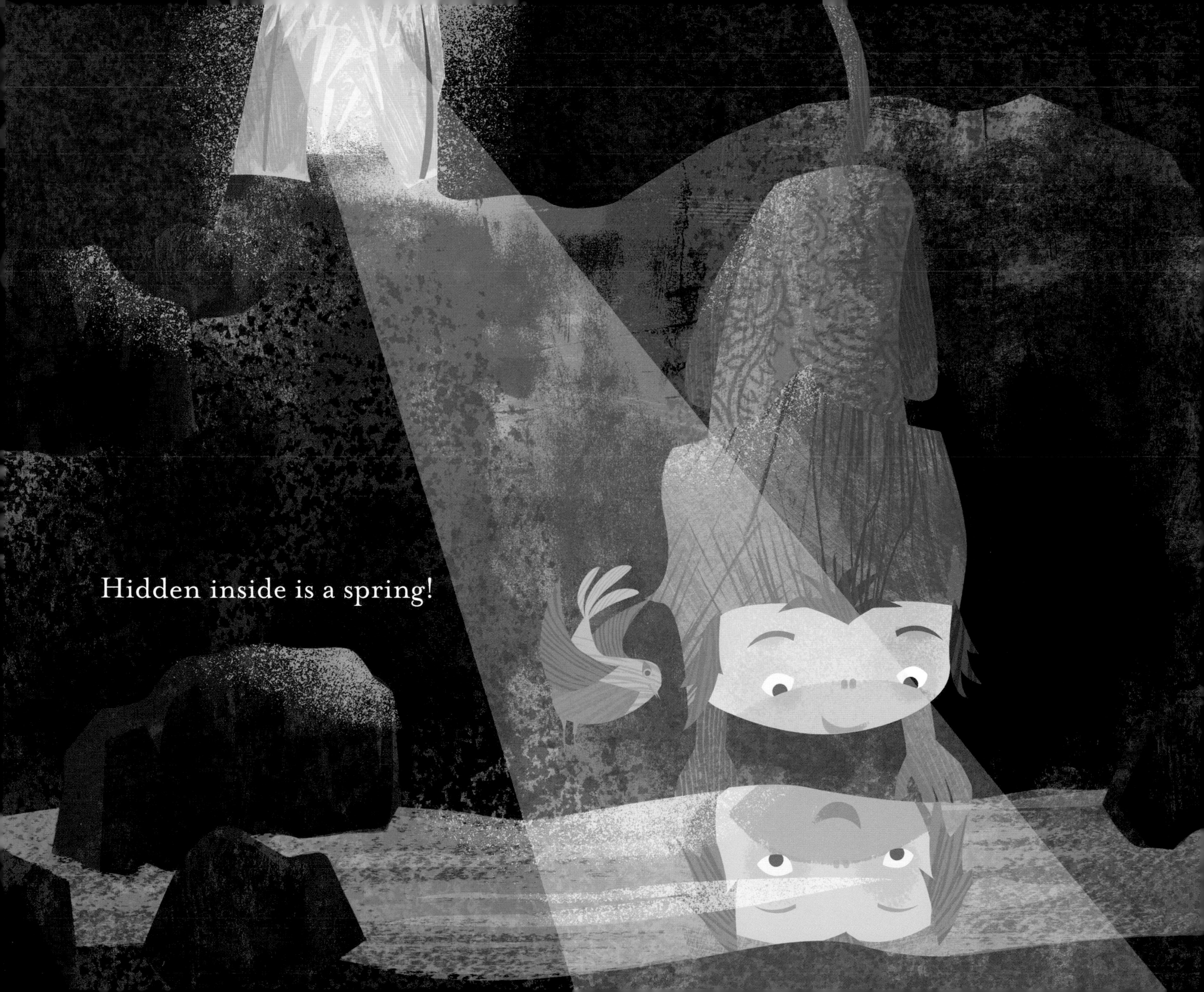

Hidden inside is a spring!

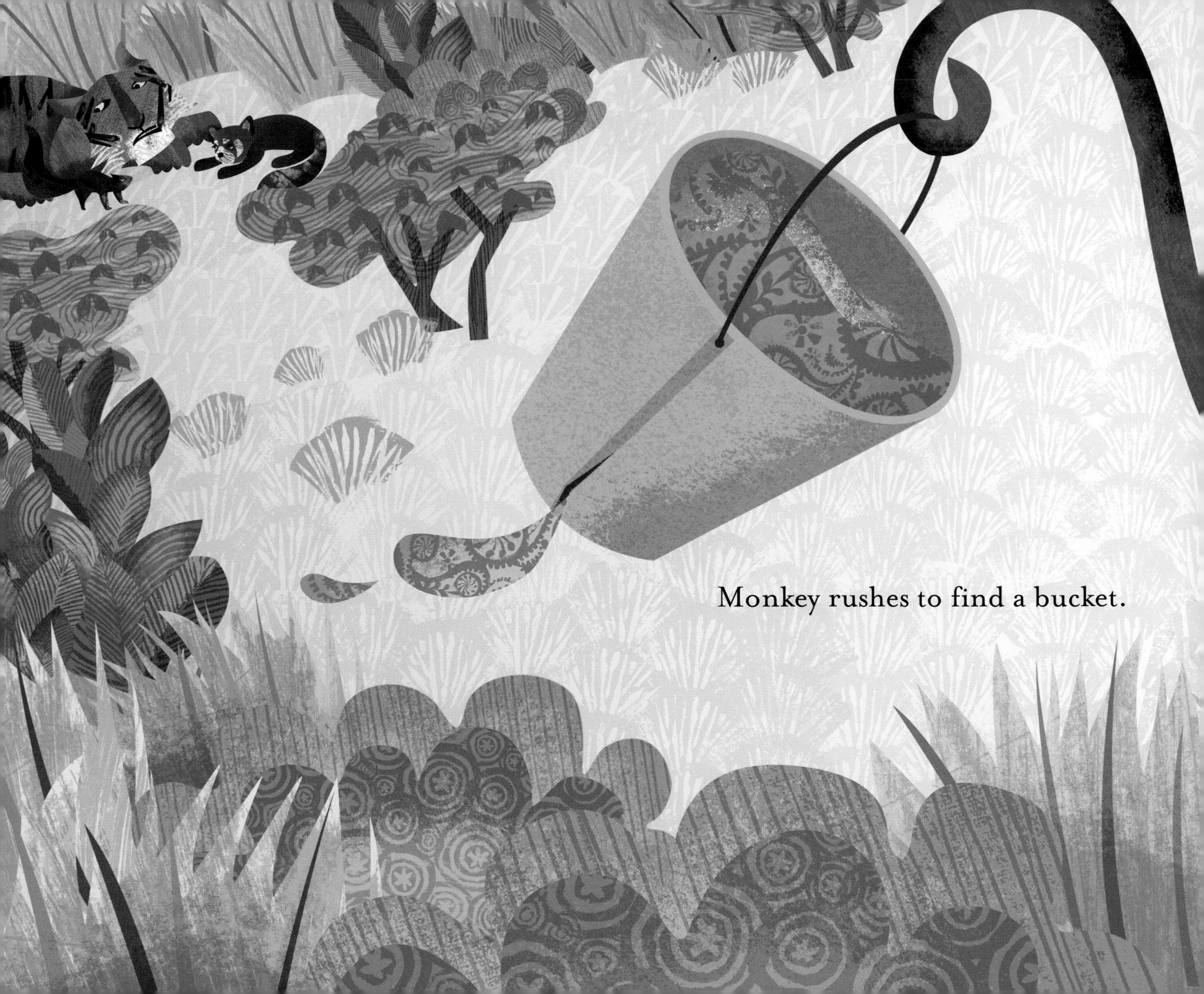

Monkey rushes to find a bucket.

He fills it and heads back
up the mountain
toward Peacock.

"Where did you find this wonderful water?" asks Toad.

"Hidden inside a cave!"
says Monkey.

"And where are you taking this wonderful water?" asks Rabbit.

"Back up the mountain
to Peacock!" says Monkey.

"And what will you do with
this wonderful water?" asks Mongoose.

"We'll try to make it rain!"
says Monkey.

Finally Monkey reaches the top of the mountain.
He can't wait to show Peacock his bucket of water.
But when he does, it's almost empty!

Monkey is crushed.
"This leaky bucket is cursed!" he says.
"But, Monkey," says Peacock,
"look behind you!"

Yet Monkey is still worried. This beauty won't last if it doesn't rain soon.

"Monkey," says Peacock, "if you can make flowers bloom with just a few splashes of water, maybe I can make it rain after all."

So Monkey pours the last drops from his bucket on Peacock.

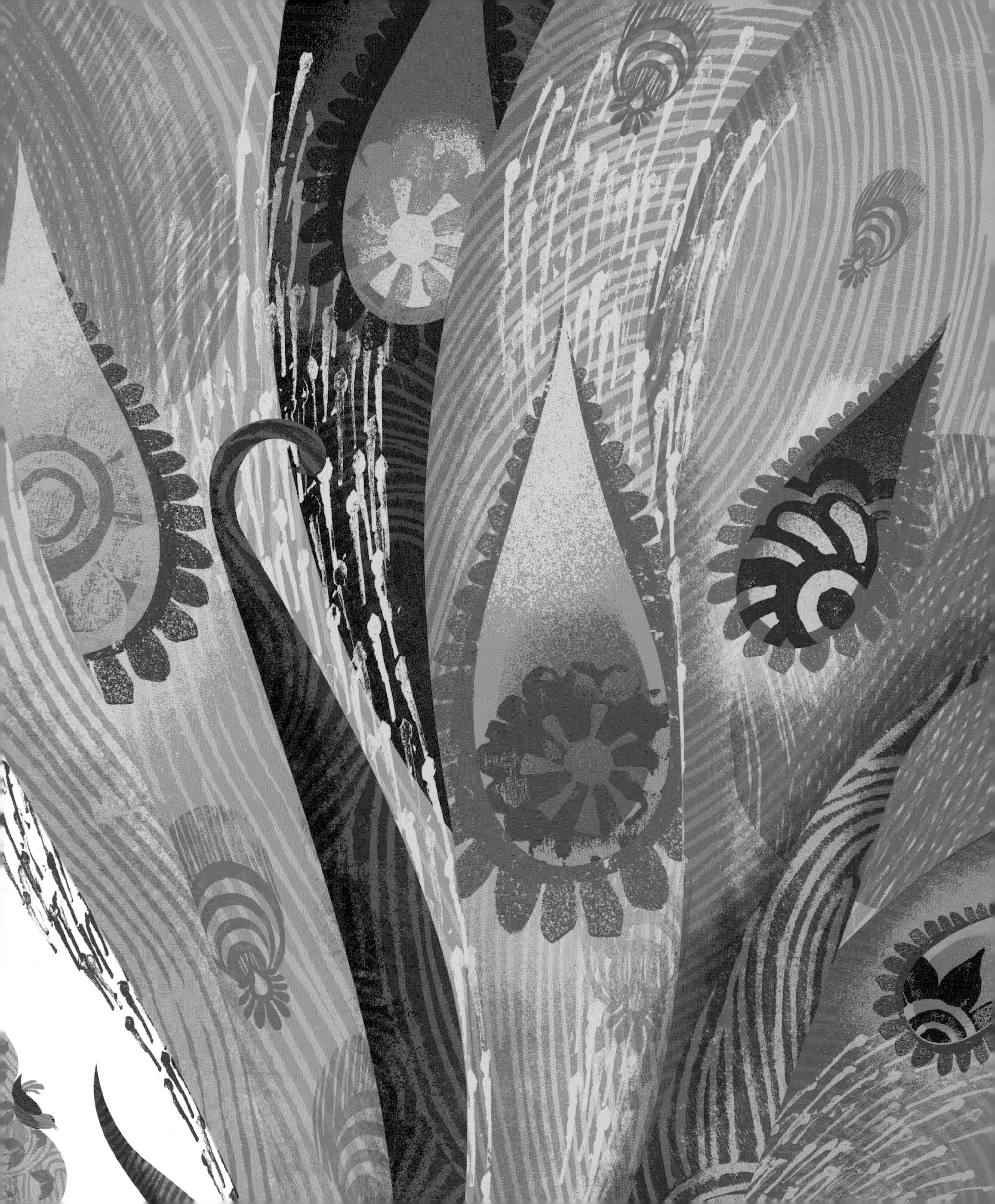

Peacock dances.

Monkey hopes.

Then the clear blue sky fills
with rumbling clouds.
And soon buckets of rain begin to fall.

"Monkey!" says Peacock. "That leaky bucket of yours . . .

". . . it was a blessing to us all!"

Afterword

Every person in this world welcomes a story. Even devout churchgoers listen at attention as the religious leader encourages good behavior to his listeners. However, the audience perks up (or even wakes up) when the speaker says, "Let me tell you a Biblical story."

The audience attends the already familiar storytelling with eagerness. These writers, Kabir Sehgal and Surishtha Sehgal, in *A Bucket of Blessings* have managed to inform the readership exquisitely of a thousand truths in just about a few hundred words.

The reader is shown that it is a blessing to be a blessing. The authors deftly show the reader that when one's intent is to help another, people whose names they will never know and faces they will never see will benefit.

This is a wonderful children's story which adults will find delightful to read.

—Dr. Maya Angelou, award-winning author of *I Know Why the Caged Bird Sings*

Authors' Note

The peacock is the national bird of India and a common motif in Indian literature, mythology, and artwork. In Hindu mythology, it can be found as a depiction of Indra, the god of rain and thunder. Today many people still believe that peacocks spread their feathers and dance when rain is imminent. Elements of the peacock's dance have been incorporated into Indian classical dances. Many years ago, a peacock charmed us with a dance while we were in India. It didn't rain, but we were blessed with a magnificent memory from which this book flowered.

Acknowledgments

We're grateful for our celestial team at Simon & Schuster and Beach Lane Books, including Jon Anderson, Allyn Johnston, and Andrea Welch, and breathtaking illustrator Jing Jing Tsong, and for our cherished friends who offered valuable input. We're thankful for the support of our loving family, Raghbir Sehgal and Kashi Sehgal.

Let's provide a Bucket of Blessings to a community in need. A portion of the proceeds from this book will go to charity: water. Learn more at charitywater.org.

To Mummy, Chambeli Gill, for planting the seed
—K.S. & S.S.

To Tien and Reid
—J.J.T.

Beach Lane Books • An imprint of Simon & Schuster Children's Publishing Division • 1230 Avenue of the Americas, New York, New York 10020 •

For information about special discounts for bulk purchases, please contact Simon & Schuster Special Sales at 1-866-506-1949 or business@simonandschuster.com. • The Simon & Schuster Speakers Bureau can bring authors to your live event. For more information or to book an event, contact the Simon & Schuster Speakers Bureau at 1-866-248-3049 or visit our website at www.simonspeakers.com. • Book design by Lauren Rille • The text for this book is set in Mrs. Eaves. • The illustrations for this book are rendered in traditional block prints in combination with digital rendering. • Manufactured in China • 0214 SCP • First Edition • 10 9 8 7 6 5 4 3 2 1 • Library of Congress Cataloging-in-Publication Data • Sehgal, Kabir. • A bucket of blessings / Kabir Sehgal and Surishtha Sehgal ; illustrated by Jing Jing Tsong.—1st ed. • p. cm. • Summary: "A picture book based on an Indian myth about a monkey who tries to save his village, and a dancing peacock that brings rain"— Provided by publisher. • ISBN 978-1-4424-5870-3 (hardcover) • ISBN 978-1-4424-5871-0 (eBook) • [1. Folklore—India.] I. Sehgal, Surishtha. II. Tsong, Jing Jing, ill. III. Title. • PZ8.1.S4543Bu 2014 • 398.20954—dc23 • [E] • 2012027500